The World of Emily Windsnap

Shona Finds Her Voice

The World of Emily Windsnap

Shona Finds Her Voice

Liz Kessler

illustrated by Joanie Stone

CANDLEWICK PRESS

*Dedicated to everyone who has ever been
too shy to share their talents. I hope this
book helps you come out of your shell.*
LK

For my est end—Amber
JS

Text copyright © 2022 by Liz Kessler
Illustrations copyright © 2022 by Joanie Stone

First edition 2022

Library of Congress Catalog Card Number 2021953145
ISBN 978-1-5362-1523-6 (hardcover)
ISBN 978-1-5362-2555-6 (paperback)

22 23 24 25 26 27 APS 10 9 8 7 6 5 4 3 2 1

Printed in Humen, Dongguan, China

This book was typeset in Stempel Schneidler.
The illustrations were created digitally.

Candlewick Press
99 Dover Street
Somerville, Massachusetts 02144

www.candlewick.com

CONTENTS

CHAPTER ONE
Off to School

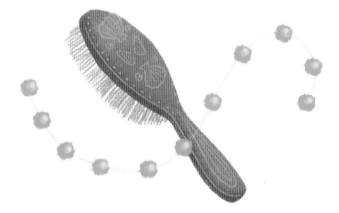

It was Monday morning, and Shona Silkfin was getting ready for school. "Ninety-eight, ninety-nine, one hundred," she said as she brushed her long hair.

Shona's mom swam by. "Are you almost ready?" she asked.

"I still have to polish my tail," Shona replied.

Shona's mom looked outside. "There's a dolphin train coming by," she said. "If you hurry, you can catch a ride to school with them."

"That's OK," Shona said. "I'd rather swim."

Five minutes later, she was on her way
to Shiprock School. Shona liked to swim.
She loved the feeling of zooming through
the water with a flick of her tail.

But there was something she liked
even more.

Singing!

Shona would sing all day if she could.

There was just one problem: she was afraid to sing in front of other people. She worried they might laugh at her or say she wasn't a good singer. So Shona never sang in front of anyone.

That morning she sang all the way to school, but made sure to stop before anyone heard her.

CHAPTER TWO
A Talent Show

At school, the merkids were crowding around the notice board.

"What is everyone looking at?" Shona asked Senara.

Senara swished her tail. "There's going to be a talent show at school next week!" she said.

"A talent show?" Shona asked. "That sounds like fun."

"But that's not even the best part," Senara said.

"It isn't?"

Senara shook her head. "It will be judged by Neptune himself!"

"Neptune?" Shona repeated. "The king of the oceans?"

"Yes! Look!"

Shona read the notice:

We are holding a show
for King Neptune.
If you have a talent, now is
the time to share it at this
once-in-a-lifetime event.
All contestants can bring
one guest. The winner
will meet the king!
Sign up here.

Shona felt her heart thump inside her. Meeting King Neptune was the most exciting thing she could imagine.

But the only talent she had was singing.

BOOKS

We are holding a show for King Neptune. If you have a talent, now the time to share it at th once-in-a-lifetime even. All contestants can brir one guest. The winne: will meet the king! Sign up here.

And singing in front of her whole school was the scariest thing she could imagine!

"Too bad I don't have any talents," she said to Senara.

Before Senara could reply, Shona swam away to her first class.

But all anyone could talk about was the talent show. It seemed like everyone was planning to perform.

Everyone except Shona.

Lyla was going

to do a dance.

Briny was going

to recite a poem.

Dillon was going to do an acrobatic act with ropes.

Everyone kept asking one another: "What are you going to do in the talent show?"

And Shona was the only one who
didn't have an answer.

CHAPTER THREE
Best Friends

After school, Shona swam to Rainbow Rocks. She was meeting her best friend, Emily Windsnap, at sunset.

While she waited, she sat on the edge of a rock and flicked her tail in the water. She sang to herself as she combed her hair with her hands. She was so lost in her song that she didn't notice Emily approaching.

"Hey!" Emily said as she swam over to the rock. With a flip of her tail, she sat next to Shona.

"Hi!" Shona smiled at her best friend.

"Did you hear that sound?" Emily asked.

"What sound?"

"I don't know. It stopped when I got here, but it was beautiful. It sounded like the ocean was singing a lullaby to the sun."

Shona laughed. "No. I definitely didn't hear that! Are you sure you're not imagining things?"

Emily laughed, too. "I guess I must have been. Come on, let's swim."

Shona was still combing through her hair. "Don't wait for me. I still have to get out these knots."

Emily slipped off the rock and into the water.

As Shona smoothed her hair, she began to sing again.

Emily was just about to dive under the water when she stopped.

"It was you!" she said.

CHAPTER FOUR
A Beautiful Voice

Shona jumped, slipping off the rock and into the water.

When she bobbed back up, Emily was grinning at her. "The beautiful song," Emily said. "It was you!"

Shona stared at her. "Really?"

"Really!" Emily said. "I can't believe I never knew what a good singer you are!"

"I've never sung in front of anyone before," Shona said.

"Well, you should because your
singing is SWISHY!" Emily said.

Swishy was their special word.

"Will you do it again?" Emily asked.

Shona looked around. There was no
one else in sight.

So Shona perched on the rock and
sang, and Emily listened.

When Shona finished, Emily clapped

so hard she splashed water everywhere.

Shona smiled. But suddenly she stopped smiling and looked sad.

"I wish I were braver," she said.

"Why?" Emily asked.

Shona told her about the talent show. "I could never sing in front of the whole school," she said. "Or in front of King Neptune!"

"Why not?"

Shona shook her head. "I'd be too scared. I just couldn't do it."

"Look how much your singing made me smile and clap and cheer! That should tell you something," Emily said.

"It tells me I can sing in front of my best friend," Shona admitted. "But you don't go to my school, so you wouldn't even be there!"

Emily frowned.

They were quiet for a moment. Then Shona's tail twitched.

"Wait!"

CHAPTER FIVE
Decision Time

"The announcement said that everyone who performs a talent can bring a guest. So if I enter, you COULD come!"

Emily grinned. "So I can be there to cheer you on!"

Shona still looked worried, though.

"What are you scared of?" Emily asked.

Shona shrugged. "That people will laugh at me, I guess. Or tell me I'm bad or—"

"Don't think about anyone else. Don't even look at them," Emily said. "Just look at me when you sing. Forget about everyone else and sing, like you just did."

"You really think I can do it?" Shona asked.

"I know you can do it! I used to worry about having a tail and being different from other kids. But since we've been friends,

I don't worry about what other people think. Having a best friend has made me realize that someone likes me just the way I am."

"That's how I feel, too," Shona said.

"So think about that if you get nervous. You can do it, Shona. I know you can."

Shona paused for a moment. Then she said, "OK. I'll do it!"

CHAPTER SIX
The Big Day

It was the day of the talent show, and

Shona was very nervous. She was hiding

in the wings, peeking out at the audience.

Then it was her turn.

There were so many people looking at the stage, waiting for her! Her tail started shaking.

Then she spotted Emily in the crowd.

She smiled and gave Shona two thumbs up.

"I can do this," Shona told herself.

She swam onto the stage, cleared her throat, and began to sing. She pretended she was sitting on a rock, singing to just her best friend. She sang and sang and sang.

When she finished, the room was
quiet. "Oh, no," Shona thought. "They
hated it. I was awful. Why did I do this?"

And then—

The crowd started clapping and cheering. They loved it!

Shona swam over to Emily.

"I think they liked it," Shona said.

"They didn't *like* it," Emily replied.
"They *loved* it!"

At the end of the show, dolphins pulled a chariot to the stage. Inside was King Neptune!

King Neptune said, "I now announce that the winner of the talent show is . . . Shona Silkfin!"

Shona couldn't believe it.

She swam up to the stage, where King
Neptune handed her a golden seashell.

"Thank you, Your Majesty," Shona said.

Then her classmates crowded around her, telling her what a good singer she was. Emily was in the middle of the group, cheering and laughing and splishing and splashing with the others.

"Thank you for helping me be brave," Shona said to Emily.

"That's what best friends are for," Emily replied.

Later that day, as she swam with her friends, Shona knew that she would never be afraid to sing again—no matter who was around to hear her!

And she sang at the top of her voice all the way home.